TJ

MATT

YUCK

YUCK'S SLIME MONSTER
AND
YUCK'S GROSS PARTY

Illustrated by Nigel Baines

www.yuckweb.com

FOR
SLIME MONSTERS:

Venetia   Ingrid
           You
   Geoff   Kate
       Kat   Jo   Elisa
Margaret   Heather

SIMON AND SCHUSTER

First published in Great Britain in 2007
by Simon & Schuster UK Ltd
A CBS COMPANY
Africa House 64–78 Kingsway London WC2B 6AH

Text © Matthew Morgan and David Sinden 2007
Cover and inside illustrations © Nigel Baines 2007

5 7 9 10 8 6 4

A CIP catalogue record for this book is
available from the British Library

ISBN-13: 978-1-4169-1094-7

Printed and bound in Great Britain by
Cox & Wyman Ltd, Reading, Berkshire

www.simonsays.co.uk
www.yuckweb.com

There was a boy so disgusting they called him Yuck

YUCK'S SLIME MONSTER

"Yuck, look what you've done!"

Polly Princess stood in Yuck's bedroom doorway clutching her *GLITTERGIRL* magazine. The pages were sticky and sloppy and covered in slime.

"It wasn't me," Yuck said. "I didn't touch your silly magazine." He was lying on his bed reading *OINK*. He turned the page...

THE SLIME MONSTER ROARED. GREAT GOBS OF SLIME SPEWED FROM ITS LIPS.
"IT'S THE SLIME MONSTER!" EVERYONE SCREAMED. "RUN FOR YOUR LIVES!"
RUN!

Polly whacked Yuck with her slimy copy of *GLITTERGIRL*. "Don't you dare touch my magazine again!"

"But it wasn't me."

"Then who was it?"

Yuck got out of bed and put *OINK* in his school bag.

"It must have been the Slime Monster," he said. Yuck held his arms out in front of him like a Slime Monster and stomped in a circle.

"There's no such thing as a Slime Monster," Polly said. "It was you and your slugs."

She opened the lid of Yuck's desk and peered inside. It was full of slugs.

"Hey, get your nose out of Slime City!"

Polly picked out a slug, threw it on the floor and...

"Stop! Don't!" Yuck yelled.

Polly trod on the slug.

SQUIDGE!

Polly raced out of the room.

Yuck looked at the squashed slug on his carpet. He scooped it up. Slime was leaking from the slug's body.

"Are you alive?" he said, stroking it.

The slug's antennae twitched feebly.

"You'll be OK. I'll fix you," Yuck said. "And then we'll fix Polly for what she did!"

Yuck raced downstairs with the slug in his hand.

Polly was waiting at the front door. "Hurry up, Yuck! I don't want to be late for school."

Yuck dashed past her and into the kitchen. He fetched the First Aid box from the shelf in the corner, took out a bandage and wrapped it around the slug.

Mum was putting the breakfast things away. "What have you got there, Yuck?" she asked.

"My slug," Yuck told her. "His name's Hero. I'm making him better."

Yuck slipped the bandaged slug into his bag and left for school with Polly.

He arrived ten minutes late. Mrs Wagon the Dragon was already pacing up and down at the front of the classroom.

Yuck opened the door quietly.

"Who's going to be in charge of Cuddly Corner this week?" the Dragon asked, pointing her umbrella.

Schoolie Julie put her hand up. "Me, Miss, please, Miss!"

Ben Bong put his hand up. "Me, Miss!"

Yuck crept along the floor on all fours, past the line of desks.

"Late AGAIN, Yuck!" the Dragon said.

"Sorry Miss," Yuck said, "there was an emergency."

The Dragon kicked Yuck's bottom, booting him to the back of the room.

He landed on his chair next to Little Eric.

Yuck sneaked the slug from his bag, unravelled its bandage and showed it to Little Eric.

"What happened?" Little Eric whispered.

"Polly squashed him. But he's going to be OK," Yuck said. "His name's Hero."

"What's THAT you've got?" the Dragon boomed.

Yuck looked up. The Dragon was pointing her umbrella towards him.

"My slug, Miss," he said.

"Get it out of here at once! You're not to bring animals to class!"

"But Miss—"

The Dragon poked Yuck with her umbrella.

"If you want to play with animals then you can look after Cuddly Corner!"

"But, Miss," Yuck said. "Cuddly Corner isn't any fun. There's only a hamster, and all it does is go round and round in its wheel. I like slugs and snails and worms and snakes."

The Dragon whacked Yuck's desk with her umbrella. "Every day this week, before and after school, you're to clean the hamster's cage, give it some food and change its water!"

"But Miss, I—"

"No buts! All week you're to get to school early and leave last."

Yuck groaned.

"Now, face the front everyone. It's time for your maths test!"

Yuck straightened Hero out, bandaged him up and slipped him back into his bag.

He pulled out his copy of *OINK* and opened it inside his maths book, to read more about the Slime Monster.

Yuck decided that when he was EMPEROR OF EVERYTHING he would rename Cuddly Corner SLIME ZONE. Inside, the walls would be green and slimy. A Slime Monster would live there. And every lunchtime Yuck would let it out to slime the school...

At the end of the day he took the key from the hook marked Cuddly Corner and walked to a hut at the edge of the playground. He undid the padlock on the door and went inside.

The hut smelled of hamster. A whirring sound was coming from a cage on a table in the corner. The hamster was running in its wheel.

Yuck peered through the bars of the cage and the hamster hopped down to see him.

"Haven't you got anyone to play with, Hammie?" Yuck asked.

The hamster twitched its whiskers.

"Do you want to have some fun?"

Hammie's whiskers twitched again.

"Then let's build a SLIME MACHINE!"
Yuck said.

Hammie squeaked happily.

Yuck had never built a slime machine
before, but he'd seen the one in *OINK*.

He opened the cage and took Hammie
out, then fetched Hero from his bag. Yuck
unwrapped the soggy bandage and his slug
started sliming across the table.

The hamster gave
the slug a sniff.

"Hammie, this is
Hero. Hero, this is
Hammie," Yuck said.

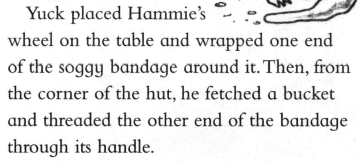

Yuck placed Hammie's
wheel on the table and wrapped one end
of the soggy bandage around it. Then, from
the corner of the hut, he fetched a bucket
and threaded the other end of the bandage
through its handle.

He tied both ends of the bandage together to make a loop.

"THIS is our slime machine!" he said.

Hammie hopped into the wheel.

"That's it, Hammie, you're going to be the engine. The bandage will be the conveyor belt that carries the slime."

Yuck placed Hero on the conveyor belt.

"Hero, you're going to be the slime-maker."

Yuck borrowed a lettuce leaf from Hammie's bowl and hung it up on a piece of string.

When Hero saw the lettuce, he began sliming along the conveyor belt towards it.

"Now run, Hammie, run," Yuck said.

As Hammie ran, the wheel turned and the conveyor belt started to move. Hero slimed forwards, trying to reach the lettuce. But the conveyor belt was going the other way, carrying his slug slime down to the bucket.

Yuck watched as the slime dripped...

plop! plop!

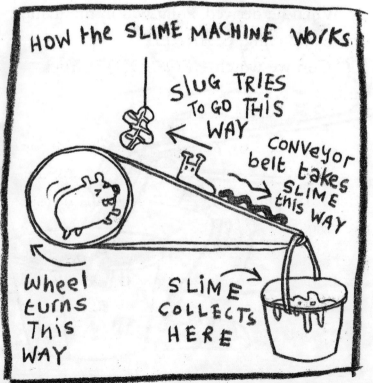

HOW the SLIME MACHINE works.

SLUG TRIES TO GO THIS WAY

CONVeyor belt takes SLIME this WAY

Wheel turns This WAY

SLIME COLLECTS HERE

He dipped his finger into the bucket. The slime was cold and slippery.

PLOP! PLOP! PLOP!

With Hammie running happily in the wheel, and Hero sliming happily on the conveyor belt, Yuck crept out.

"Good night, Hammie. Good night, Hero," he said.

He locked the door and went home.

When he arrived, Polly was in the living room watching *SPARKLE*.

"Can we watch *GROSSOUT*?" Yuck asked.

"I was here first," Polly said.

"But I had to look after Cuddly Corner."

"Cuddly Corner? Why are you looking after Cuddly Corner – or did you run out of slugs to play with?"

Polly picked a crusty glob of Hero's slime from her shoe and flicked it at Yuck.

He caught the slime and wiped it on her hair, then ran to his room to read *OINK*.

The next morning, Yuck was first to school.

"Rockits!" he said, opening the door to Cuddly Corner. The bucket was FULL of slime. All night Hammie had been turning the wheel and all night Hero had been sliming on the conveyor belt.

The slime machine had worked!

"Well done, Hammie! Well done Hero!"

He placed Hero on the table beside the cage, took Hammie out of the wheel and gave them both some lettuce and fresh water. Then he untied the bandage, rolled it up and hid it in the corner.

"I'll see you later. Have fun," he said.

Yuck headed outside carrying the bucket full of slime.

At break-time he slipped a handful of slime down Little Eric's shirt.

Little Eric felt something gooey running down his back.

"Urrgghh!" he said. "What's that?"

"Slime!" Yuck told him. He showed Little Eric the bucket.

"Let me have a go," Little Eric said. He took a big scoop of slime and flicked it at Yuck.

Yuck flicked a handful of slime back at Little Eric.

Then they both took another scoop and catapulted slime into the air.

"It's raining slime!" Yuck said.

At that moment, Polly Princess and Juicy Lucy skipped out of the canteen into the playground.

"URRGGHH!" Polly shrieked, as slime rained down on her hair.

Lucy looked up and slime dropped in her mouth. "AARRGGHH!" she screamed.

Yuck and Little Eric were giggling.

But, just then, the Dragon marched over. "What's going on here?" she boomed, seeing Polly and Lucy covered in slime.

"It was Yuck!" Polly said.

Little Eric stood in front of the bucket to hide it.

"It wasn't us, Miss," Yuck said.

"Then who was it?" the Dragon asked.

"It was the Slime Monster, Miss," Yuck said. "It was horrible, like a human being, but slimier and scarier. And it walked funny, Miss – like this…"

Yuck held his arms out in front of him like a Slime Monster and stomped in a circle.

"What nonsense," the Dragon said.

"There's no such thing as a Slime Monster, Miss," Polly told her.

"I want everyone to get cleaned up immediately," the Dragon said. "When I find out who did this they'll be in BIG TROUBLE."

But for the rest of lunchtime, Yuck and Little Eric went hunting for more slugs.

After school they took them all to Cuddly Corner.

Yuck fetched the bandage from the corner of the hut and looped one end of it around Hammie's wheel. This time he placed TWO buckets on the floor, and threaded the other end of the bandage through both their handles.

He tied the ends together and the conveyor belt was ready.

"Wow!" Little Eric said. "A slime machine!"

Yuck placed Hero on the conveyor belt then added the extra slugs behind him in a line.

"More slugs means more slime!" Yuck said.

Hammie hopped into the wheel and started running. The wheel turned, the conveyor belt moved and the slime machine began sliming.

plop! plop! plop! SPLAT!

Hammie was running at full speed.

"That's it," Yuck said. "Keep it up."

He made sure all the slugs were in a neat line and copying Hero at the front.

"The slime will be ready in the morning," Yuck said to Little Eric. "Get here early."

They left and locked the door.

The next morning, Yuck and Little Eric rushed to school. They opened the door of Cuddly Corner and saw the TWO buckets full of slime.

The machine had been sliming all night.

"Well done, Hammie," Yuck said. "Well done, Hero. Well done, everyone!"

He took Hammie out of the wheel and placed Hero and the other slugs beside the cage, giving them lettuce and fresh water.

"We'll see you later. Have fun."

Yuck left carrying one bucket full of slime. Little Eric carried the other.

That lunchtime, Yuck and Little Eric poured the slime along the school corridor. They skidded up and down.

"Rockits!" Yuck said. "Slimeboarding!"

Fartin Martin and Tom Bum ran over.

"Slime!" Tom Bum said. "Brilliant!"

"Let's have a go!" Fartin Martin said.

But at that moment, Polly and Lucy came out of Miss Fortune's classroom, each carrying a stack of books. Clip–Clop Chloe, Megan the Mouth and Madison Snake came after them.

"Mind out of the way!" Fartin Martin called.

"Arrgghh!" Polly screamed.

"Help!" Lucy screamed.

Fartin Martin and Tom Bum skidded towards them.

WHOOSH!

The books tumbled as everyone slid down the corridor and landed with a…

SPLAT!

Just as they struggled to their feet, Frank the Tank came running out of the toilets. He slipped on the slime and slid down the corridor like a bowling ball.

CRASH!

He knocked everyone down like skittles.

The Dragon heard the noise and dashed out of her classroom.

"What's going on here?" she boomed. She slipped and landed on her bottom. "Where IS all this slime coming from?"

"It's the Slime Monster, Miss," Yuck said.

"Slime Monster!" everyone shrieked.

"W-w-what's a Slime Monster?" Frank the Tank asked.

"It's like a human being, but slimier and scarier," Yuck said. "And it walks funny — like this…"

Yuck held his arms out in front of him like a Slime Monster and stomped in a circle.

"He's lying. There's no such thing as a Slime Monster," Polly said.

The Dragon clambered to her feet. She scowled at Yuck. "If I find out this has anything to do with you, you'll be in BIG TROUBLE. Go and get a mop from Mr Sweep and clean this up. You too, Eric."

"But it wasn't us, Miss," Little Eric said. "It was—"

"I'll hear no more nonsense about Slime Monsters!" the Dragon said.

Yuck and Little Eric giggled as the Dragon squelched back into her classroom.

"Is there really a Slime Monster sliming the school?" Frank the Tank asked.

"Yes," Yuck said. "If you TOUCH the Slime Monster, your skin melts."

"If you HEAR the Slime Monster, your earwax melts," Little Eric said.

"And if you SEE the Slime Monster, you have to… RUN FOR YOUR LIFE!"

Yuck and Little Eric laughed all the way
to Mr Sweep the caretaker's cupboard.
There, beside the mop, they found more
buckets.

After school, Yuck, Fartin Martin, Tom
Bum and Little Eric went hunting for slugs
again, filling their pockets before heading
to Cuddly Corner.

Yuck fetched the bandage, and this time
threaded the conveyor belt through TEN
buckets.

"Cool! A slime machine!" Tom Bum said.
"Brilliant!" Fartin Martin said.

Yuck placed Hero at the front of the
conveyor belt. Everyone took the slugs from
their pockets and lined them up behind
him. Hammie hopped into the wheel.

"Run, Hammie, run!"

The machine began sliming.

PLOP! PLOP! PLOP! PLOP!
SPLAT! PLOP! PLOP!
Gurgle! SPLAT! PLOP!

"We'll collect the slime in the morning!" Yuck said.

The next morning, Yuck, Fartin Martin, Tom Bum and Little Eric arrived at school early. They ran to Cuddly Corner.

Inside were TEN buckets FULL of slime!

"Well done, Hammie," Yuck said. "Well done, Hero. Well done, everyone!"

He placed Hammie and the slugs in a huddle and gave them lettuce and fresh water. Then he took the bandage off the machine and hid it.

Yuck, Fartin Martin, Tom Bum and Little Eric picked up the buckets full of slime and set to work.

"Let's let the Slime Monster loose," Yuck said.

At lunchtime they slimed the classrooms. They slimed windows and white boards, door handles and desks, books and bags.

When the Dragon sat on her chair it squelched. She opened her umbrella as slime dripped from the ceiling.

They slimed the toilet seats and sinks.

They slimed the pizzas and puddings in the canteen.

"There's a Slime Monster on the loose!" Ben Bong cried, about to eat a spoonful of slime.

Everyone ran out to the playground.

But the playground was slimy too!

Megan the Mouth slipped off the climbing frame and Spoilt Jessica whooshed down the slide.

Mr Reaper the headmaster was on playground patrol.

"Where IS all this slime coming from?" he asked.

"It's the Slime Monster," everyone said. "The Slime Monster's come to get us!"

"There's no such thing as a Slime Monster!" Polly cried. She was sitting up in a tree with Lucy, trying to escape from the slime.

Meanwhile, Yuck, Fartin Martin, Tom Bum and Little Eric were collecting more slugs.

"Let's use snails, too," Yuck said, filling his bag. "We're going to make the biggest slime machine EVER."

After school, Yuck borrowed more bandages from Nurse Payne's sickroom and went to Cuddly Corner. He tied all the bandages together to make a super-long conveyor belt and unwound it round the room – up and down and back and forth.

Fartin Martin, Tom Bum and Little Eric arrived carrying armfuls of slugs and snails.

"We need lots," Yuck said, emptying his bag.

Fartin Martin emptied the cap from off his head. Tom Bum emptied his shoes. Little Eric emptied his pants.

Slugs and snails rolled out over the floor – hundreds of them!

Yuck, Fartin Martin, Tom Bum and Little Eric loaded them onto the conveyor belt.

"You go at the front, Hero," Yuck said, placing Hero nearest the lettuce. "Show everyone what to do."

"We'll need more buckets," Fartin Martin said.

They stacked buckets and boxes and pots and jars all around the hut to collect the slime.

Hammie hopped into the wheel and began running.

"That's it, Hammie," Yuck said.

The conveyor belt started to move. The slugs and snails started sliding along it, one after the other. The slime machine began sliming.

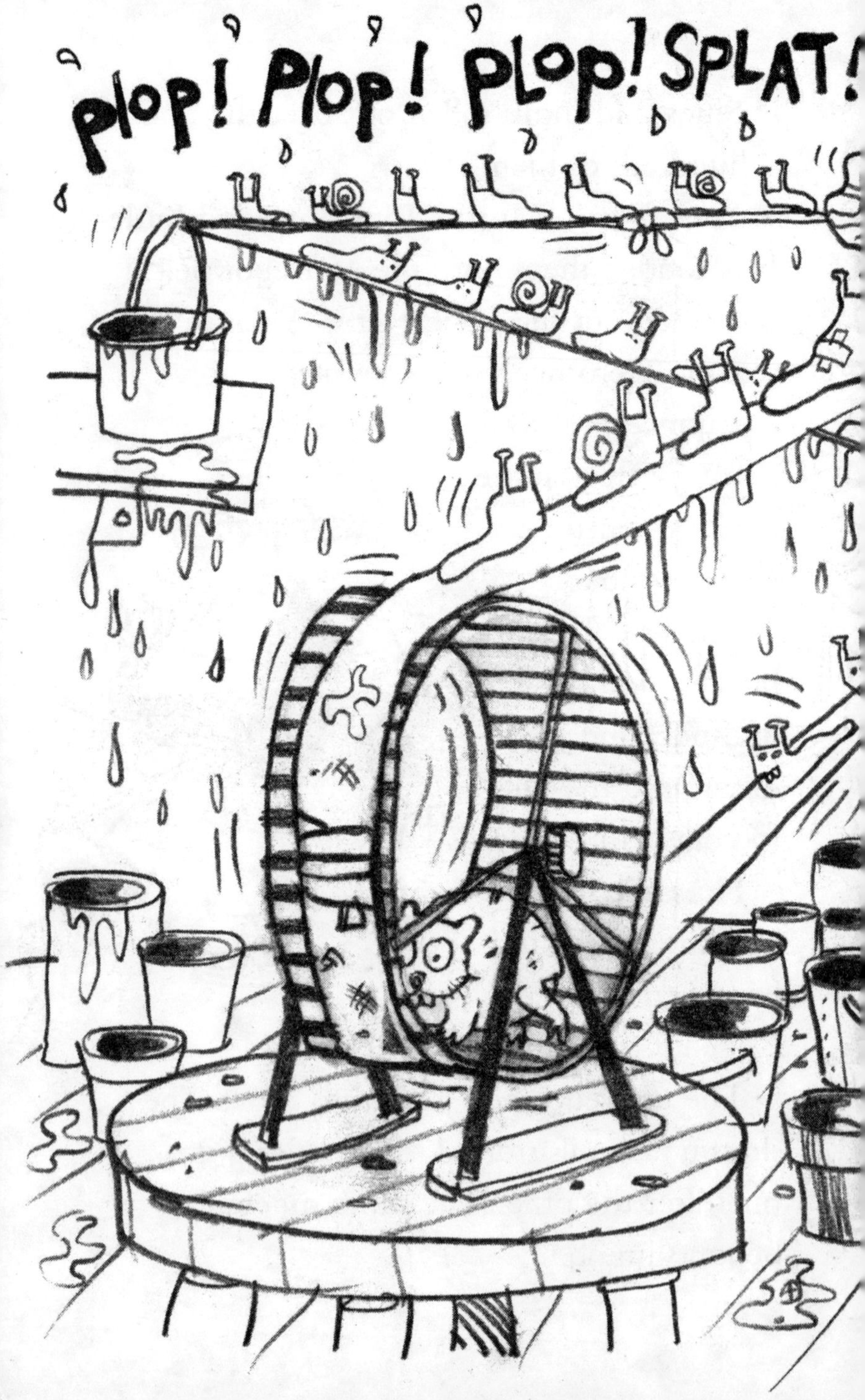
PLOP! PLOP! PLOP! SPLAT!

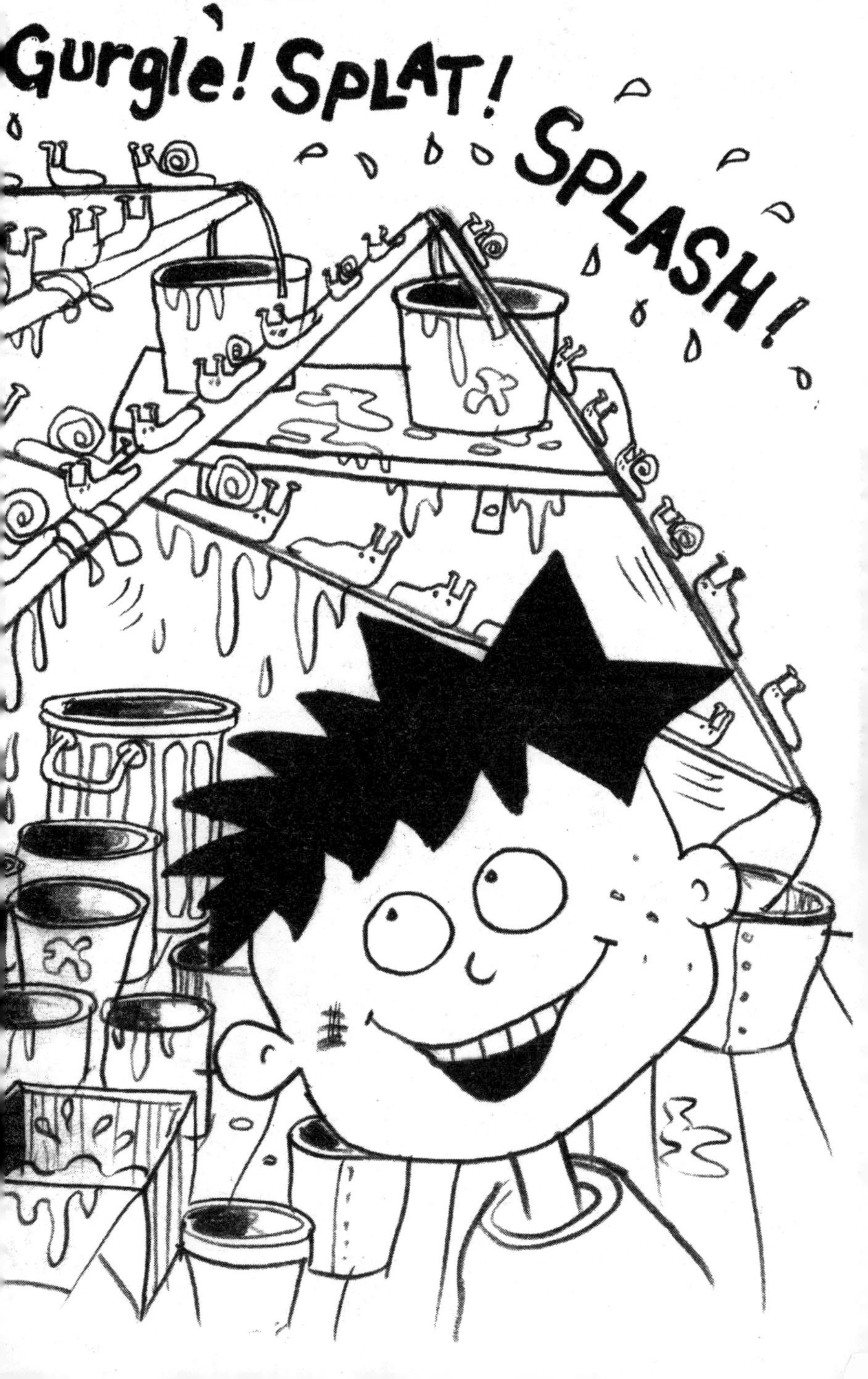

Gurgle! SPLAT! SPLASH!

"Good night, Hammie. Good night, Hero. Good night, everyone."

Yuck, Fartin Martin, Tom Bum and Little Eric clambered through the bandages and out of the hut. Yuck locked the door.

"We'll collect the slime in the morning," he said. "There'll be loads of it – our very own Slime Zone!"

But when Yuck got home, Polly was waiting for him.

"I know what really happened at school today," she said. "There's no such thing as a Slime Monster! And now I have the proof!"

From behind her back she pulled out Yuck's copy of *OINK*.

She opened it to the page with the Slime Monster. "The Slime Monster's just a story. It's YOU who's been sliming the school!"

"Give me back my *OINK*!" Yuck said, trying to grab his comic from her.

But Polly stuffed it into her bag. "I'm telling on you. You're going to be in BIG TROUBLE."

The next morning, when Yuck left for school, Polly had already gone.

By the time Yuck got there, the Dragon was waiting for him at the school gates. In her hand was his copy of *OINK*.

Standing beside her was Polly.

"You're coming with me," the Dragon said to Yuck, dragging him by his ear to the Reaper's office.

Fartin Martin, Tom Bum and Little Eric were already inside.

"I think you have some explaining to do," the Reaper said.

He marched them all to assembly.

Meanwhile, Polly went to Cuddly
Corner to find out what Yuck had been up
to. From inside, she could hear strange
sounds.

**Gurgle! SPLAT!
PLop! SPLASH!**

Something was leaking out under the
door – slime!

Polly turned the handle, but the door was
locked. She rattled and tugged.

Then all at once the door burst open…

A river of slime poured out from Cuddly
Corner, knocking Polly to the
ground. It covered
her from head to toe.

Slime dripped
from her hair and
oozed from her
clothes. She could
feel slugs in her
socks and snails
in her pants.

Hammie the hamster ran across her slimy face.

Hero slimed across her lips.

"Help!" she cried, trying to get up. "HELP!"

But no one heard her. Everyone was in assembly.

"There is no such thing as a Slime Monster," the Reaper was saying to the school. "There is no reason for any of you to be afraid. And now we have the proof!"

The Reaper held up Yuck's copy of *OINK*, opening it at the page with the Slime Monster.

"The Slime Monster is a lie," the Reaper said. "It's just a story in a comic belonging to a naughty boy."

He stared straight at Yuck. "Is this yours?"

"Can I have it back, please?" Yuck asked.

"It's you, Yuck! You're the one who's sliming the school!" the Reaper yelled.

Everyone went quiet.

Yuck looked at the Reaper. "I told you, Sir. It isn't me." Then Yuck looked around the room. "It's the Slime Monster!"

Everyone gasped.

The Reaper's face turned red with rage. He shouted at Yuck: "THERE IS NO SUCH THING AS A SLIME MONSTER!"

At that moment the doors at the back of assembly banged open.

Everyone turned.

Standing in the doorway was a THING – like a human being, but slimier and scarier. It walked slowly forwards, its arms held out in front of it, slime dripping from its body and squelching under its feet.

It tried to speak – "HELP!" – but great globs of slime spewed from its lips.

"It's the Slime Monster!" everyone screamed.

Yuck picked up his copy of *OINK* and slipped it into his pocket. He was laughing. "Run for your lives!"

YUCK'S GROSS PARTY

Polly Princess stirred the cake mixture in the bowl.

Yuck looked at it. It was gooey and chocolatey. He scooped out a sticky dollop and stuffed it into his mouth.

"Hands off!" Polly said. "It's mine."

She bashed him with the spoon.

"Go away!" she said. "It's MY birthday cake for MY birthday party. And YOU'RE not invited!"

Polly poured the cake mixture into a baking tin.

"But I like cake," Yuck said. He licked his fingers.

"Tough!" Polly said. "Because you're not getting any. And you're not coming to my birthday party!"

"Move out of the way, please, Yuck," Mum said, opening the kitchen door.

"Mum, why can't I come to Polly's party?" Yuck asked.

"Because you're gross," Polly said.

"Because last year you ate too much cake and were sick on Polly's presents," Mum told him.

Mum picked up the tin with the cake mixture and slid it into the oven.

Yuck took the mixing bowl with the leftover mixture and sneaked out of the kitchen. He crept past Dad who was blowing up party balloons, and ran up the stairs to his room. He sat on his bed, put the bowl on his head and span it round, licking it clean.

Yuck decided that when he was EMPEROR OF EVERYTHING he would have the best party ever – a GROSS PARTY! Everyone would be invited. They'd wear gross costumes and play gross games with slime and slugs and mud and maggots. They'd jump around and eat SO MUCH chocolate cake that everyone would be sick!

Yuck set to work on his plan.

At about three o'clock the doorbell rang.

It was Juicy Lucy with Little Eric.

Polly ran to greet her first guests.

"Happy Birthday, Polly," Juicy Lucy said,
stepping inside.

"What's he doing here?" Polly asked,
pointing at Little Eric.

"I'm here for the party," Little Eric said.

"But you weren't invited."

Yuck appeared at the top of the stairs.

"Not YOUR party, Polly. MY party. It's up here, Eric," he called.

Little Eric ran upstairs.

Juicy Lucy handed Polly a big present wrapped in pink paper. "I didn't know Yuck was having a party too," she said.

"Nor did I!" Polly replied.

The doorbell rang again.
It was Madison Snake.
"Happy Birthday, Polly!"
Madison Snake said. She
was carrying an even
bigger present.

"Thank you," Polly said, taking it from
her with both hands. "I'm going to open
them later."

Madison Snake and Juicy Lucy went
into the living room where Mum poured
them fizzy drinks. Polly waited by the door
as the rest of her friends arrived – Emily
Brush, Clip-Clop Chloe, Megan the
Mouth, Spoilt Jessica and the Twinkletrout,
each carrying a present.

Polly was about to close the door when… "Oh no!"

Tom Bum and Fartin Martin came walking up the path.

"We're here for the party," they said.

"You're not invited," Polly told them.

"Not YOUR party, Polly. MY party!" Yuck called from the top of the stairs.

Fartin Martin and Tom Bum ran up to Yuck's room.

"I had to hide everything," Yuck said. From his wardrobe Yuck took out three toilet rolls, a bottle of ketchup, a tube of toothpaste, a packet of Blowers' Bubblegum and a super-sized bottle of Coola Cola.

He popped a piece of bubblegum into his mouth, glugged some Coola Cola, and chewed.

BUUUUURP!

A cola-coloured bubblegum bubble expanded from Yuck's lips.

He took it out and stuck it to the wall.

"Balloons!" he said, handing everyone some gum.

They drank and chewed and burped, sticking up Bubblegum Burp Balloons.

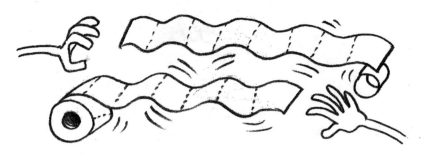

Little Eric and Tom Bum decorated the room with streamers, throwing toilet rolls back and forth. Fartin Martin squirted toothpaste onto the ceiling so that it hung down like ribbons. Yuck took the ketchup and squeezed the words GROSS PARTY on the window. In no time at all, the room was ready.

"Welcome to my party!" Yuck said.

He put on some music and the four of them drank the Coola Cola and jumped around, crashing into each other.

Downstairs, Polly was sitting in the middle of the living room surrounded by a huge pile of presents.

The ceiling thumped.

"Is Yuck having a party, too?" Clip-Clop Chloe asked.

"Not a proper one," Polly said.

Her friends sat in a circle and watched as Polly opened her presents – a matching Donna Disco skirt and top, pink lip gloss, a *SPARKLE* poster, a charm bracelet, a secret diary and a *GLITTERGIRL* annual.

Mum and Dad stood smiling in the doorway.

"Who wants to play a party game?" Polly asked.

Upstairs, Yuck, Fartin Martin, Tom Bum
and Little Eric crashed down in a big
burping heap on the floor.

"Present time!" Yuck said. From under
his bed he took out three parcels. "At my
party, everyone gets a present."

Fartin Martin got
a fat slimy slug.

"I call him THE
BEAST!" Yuck said.

Fartin Martin put
the slug under his
cap for safe keeping.

Tom Bum unwrapped
a set of plastic fangs.

"I found them in the
park," Yuck told him.

Tom Bum slipped
them into his mouth.

Little Eric unwrapped
his present.

"Brilliant, a Stink
Bomb!" he said.

Yuck's present was a small blob of chocolate cake mix that he'd been keeping on his chin. He licked it

"Let's get some food," he said.

Yuck, Fartin Martin, Tom Bum and Little Eric crept downstairs and peered round the living room door.

"Who wants to play Party Faces?" Polly was asking.

"Can I use your new lip gloss?" Juicy Lucy asked.

"I brought some glitter," the Twinkletrout said.

Polly saw Yuck at the door. "What are you doing here? You're not invited."

"We're hungry," Yuck told her, looking at the party food laid out on the table.

"Tell them to go away, Mum!"

"You can take a small plateful each and eat it upstairs," Mum said. "But don't come back for seconds."

Yuck, Little Eric, Fartin Martin and Tom Bum each piled a paper plate with crisps, sandwiches, biscuits, jelly and ice cream.

"Hang on. Where's the chocolate cake?"
Yuck asked.

"We're having it later," Polly said. "And
you're not getting any."

Yuck stuffed a bottle of Coola Cola
under his T-shirt and they ran back
upstairs.

"And now for the party games!" Yuck said.

He opened a cheese sandwich and dolloped in some jelly.

"The first game is called Spin And Be Sick."

Everyone ate their food as quickly as possible, stuffing their mouths with jelly-filled sandwiches, ice cream, biscuits and crisps. They guzzled the Coola Cola.

"Now, SPIN!" Yuck said.

Everyone stood up and began spinning.

"Faster!" Yuck called. "First to be sick is the winner."

They held their arms out and span round and round, faster and faster.

"I feel dizzy," Tom Bum said.

"I feel giddy," Fartin Martin said.

"I feel sick," Little Eric said. His stomach was gurgling. "Quick, shake me up!"

The others picked Little Eric up and shook him.

"That's it," he said. "Shake harder!"

Yuck, Fartin Martin and Tom Bum
turned Little Eric upside down.

Little Eric opened his mouth. "Here
it comes!"

BLURGH!

Sandwiches
and ice cream, jelly
and biscuits and crisps fell
with a splash onto the floor.

"I win!" Little Eric said.

Yuck handed Little Eric a prize
– a Superspy Magnifying Glass
that he'd got free with *OINK*.

Everyone gathered round and inspected
the sick.

"Is that a jam tart?" Tom Bum said. "I
didn't get a jam tart."

He picked it out and bit into it with his
plastic fangs. Jam squeezed out like blood.

"Time for our costumes!" Yuck said.

Tom Bum wrapped a towel round his
shoulders like a vampire cape. Fartin
Martin wound himself in toilet roll like a
mummy. Yuck stuck a plastic eye to his
forehead like a monster.

Little Eric put on a pair of swimming goggles from Yuck's drawer. "Is there a prize for the best costume?" he asked.

Yuck nodded. "There's a rubber scorpion for the winner."

"Then watch this," Little Eric said.

Everyone watched as Little Eric opened Yuck's desk and dipped his head in Slime City. He pulled it out, with shiny green slime dripping down his face. "I'm an alien from the planet Xarg!" he said.

The vampire, the mummy and the monster all laughed. "You look like a frog!"

Little Eric sat down — straight into his sick. "I don't care," he smiled. "This is a great party, Yuck. Much better than Polly's."

Downstairs, Polly and her friends were playing Lucky Dip, sitting in a circle around a big jar of Lucky Lollipops, each of which was wrapped in a Lucky Promise.

Polly pulled out a lollipop and unwrapped it. "You will be rich," she read.

Juicy Lucy pulled out a lollipop. "You will be famous," she read.

"My go," Megan the Mouth said.

Upstairs, Yuck took out his Disgusting Dip — a huge jar filled with writhing maggots and disgusting dares.

Fartin Martin, Tom Bum and Little Eric dipped their hands in.

"It feels warm and tickly," Tom Bum said.

He pulled out his dare – a scab on a stick. Stuck to it was a note saying LICK ME.

"It took me a month to grow that one," Yuck said.

Tom Bum held the scab on a stick like a lollipop, stuck his tongue out and gave the scab a big lick. "UURRGGHH!"

Little Eric pulled out a crisp packet saying EAT ME. Inside were Yuck's toenail clippings. He picked out a handful and chewed them. "Cheesy!"

Yuck's dare was a matchbox saying SNIFF ME. He opened it and sniffed.

"There's nothing in it!" the others said.

Yuck held it under their noses.

"PHWOOOAAARRR! What is it?"

"Cat fart," Yuck told them.

"My go," Fartin Martin said. He pulled out a little pot saying PUT ME DOWN YOUR PANTS.

Inside was a large hairy spider.

Fartin Martin pulled out the elastic of his
pants and popped the spider in.

"It tickles," he said.

He started wriggling.

"You look like you're dancing," Little
Eric said.

Little Eric, Tom Bum and Yuck stood up
and began shaking their legs and wriggling
in time with Fartin Martin, doing The
Spiderpants Dance.

In the living room, Polly's friends were whispering to each other.

"What's going on up there?" the Twinkletrout asked.

"It sounds like they're dancing again," Megan the Mouth said.

"Why can't we have dancing?" the Twinkletrout said. "I love dancing."

"So do I," Clip-Clop Chloe said, clip-clopping her feet up and down.

"Only if I choose the music," Polly told them.

Upstairs, Yuck reached under his bed and took out a rotten apple.

"This game's called Find The Maggot," he said, poking holes into the apple with a pencil.

He took a maggot from the Disgusting Dip and dropped it into one hole.

Yuck put the apple on the floor and span it round.

"There's a prize for whoever gets the maggot," he said.

Everyone took it in turns to take a bite.

On his second bite, Fartin Martin felt something crawling in his mouth. He opened wide. "I win!"

A maggot was wriggling on his tongue.

"What's the prize?" he asked.

Yuck picked up the half-eaten apple and carefully filled the remaining holes with more maggots.

"You get to eat the rest of the apple," he said, laughing.

Downstairs, Polly was dancing. "Follow me. Step to the left. Step to the right—"

She turned round. Her friends were sitting down whispering to each other.

Polly turned off the music.

"What's the matter?" she asked.

"We want to do something fun," Spoilt Jessica said.

"I know, let's do my Treasure Hunt," Polly told them.

"What's the treasure?" Spoilt Jessica asked.

"A big bar of chocolate!" Polly said.

Everyone quickly jumped up when they heard this.

"You have to hunt around the house to find it. Ready, steady, go!"

Everyone ran out of the living room, pushing past each other.

Upstairs, Yuck opened his desk and took out three slugs from Slime City. "The next game's a race," he said. "A slug race!"

He gave a slug each to Tom Bum and Little Eric. "I'm going to use Hero," he said, taking out his favourite slug. "You can use THE BEAST," he said to Fartin Martin.

Fartin Martin took the fat slimy slug from under his hat.

Yuck squeezed toothpaste in lines across the carpet to make a racetrack. He squeezed a START and FINISH line at either end. "First slug to cross the line wins a big bar of chocolate," he said.

Yuck stood on his bed and from his dusty shelf took down a giant bar of Chocoblock.

"Wow, where did you get that?" Little Eric asked.

"I found it in the cupboard under the stairs," Yuck said.

Everyone put their slugs on the START line.

"Ready! Steady! Go!"

Little Eric's slug was first away.

Hero went sideways.

Tom Bum's slug went backwards.

"Wrong way!" Tom Bum shouted.

"Come on," Little Eric cheered.

THE BEAST started eating the toothpaste.

"Not now, BEAST!" Fartin Martin said, prodding his fat slimy slug.

"You can't use your hands," Yuck said. "You're only allowed to move your slug with your nose."

At that moment, there was a knock at the door.

"Who's there?" Yuck asked.

"It's Chloe."

Yuck sat on the Chocoblock as Clip-Clop Chloe opened the door.

"Sorry to disturb you," she said, "but I'm hunting for a big bar of chocolate."

"It's not in here," Yuck said.

Clip-Clop Chloe looked at the slugs and toothpaste on the carpet.

"What are you doing?" she asked.

"We're having a party," Fartin Martin said.

"Why's Little Eric covered in slime?"

"Because it's a GROSS PARTY, the best party ever," Little Eric told her.

"It looks like fun," Clip-Clop Chloe said.

"Chloe!" Polly called from downstairs. "Where are you?"

"Got to go," Chloe said.

She closed the door and clip-clopped down the stairs.

Little Eric's slug was way out in front. He was nudging it along with his nose. Then all of a sudden his slug stopped. Little Eric had pushed it into his sick.

"I'm coming past!" Yuck said, as Hero overtook.

"No one beats THE BEAST!" Fartin Martin said. He sneezed, and THE BEAST flew over the FINISH line. "I win!"

Fartin Martin held up the Chocoblock. "Who wants a piece?"

Downstairs, Polly's friends were gathered in a huddle.

"What kind of person has a treasure hunt with no treasure?" Emily Brush whispered.

"This party is no fun at all," Spoilt Jessica said.

"I promise there was chocolate – a giant bar of Chocoblock. I hid it in the cupboard under the stairs. I promise I did," Polly said.

"Maybe we should all go home," Madison Snake whispered.

"No, please don't go! We've still got Pass the Parcel. Then after that we can have some cake!"

Polly picked up a big parcel wrapped in layer upon layer of pink paper.

"Mum," she called.

Mum came in from the kitchen and turned the music on. Everyone sat in a circle passing the parcel between them. When the music stopped, whoever was holding the parcel tore off a layer of wrapping paper.

Upstairs, Yuck fetched a bucket of mud from his wardrobe. "Who wants to play Pass the Mud?" he asked.

He put some music on and they passed the bucket round.

"When I stop the music, whoever's holding the bucket scoops out a handful of mud," Yuck said.

"This mud smells," Fartin Martin said, sniffing his fingers.

"It had dog poo in it," Yuck told him.

Little Eric scooped out a handful and sniffed it.

Tom Bum scooped out a handful and threw it at Little Eric.

Yuck scooped out a handful and threw it at Tom Bum.

At the bottom of the bucket was a prize. Little Eric pulled it out and scraped the mud off. "A bubble machine! Fantastic!"

Downstairs, Polly and her friends were
on the last layer of wrapping paper.

The music stopped and the parcel landed
on Spoilt Jessica's lap.

Carefully she unwrapped it.

"It smells," she said.

"It smells a lot," Megan the Mouth said.

The prize was brown.

Spoilt Jessica prodded it with her finger.
"IT'S DOG POO!" she screamed.

"It can't be!" Polly said. "It was supposed
to be a bubble machine!"

Upstairs, bubbles were filling Yuck's room. Everyone was leaping around, bursting them.

"Yuck!" Polly screamed, running up the stairs.

Yuck wedged a chair against his door.

"Where's my bubble machine? And where's my chocolate?" Polly shouted, rattling the handle. "Open up and give me back my prizes."

"I don't know what you're talking about, Polly," Yuck said.

Polly stomped down the stairs. "I'm telling Mum!"

But when she got to the living room, everyone had their coats on.

"No, wait," Polly told them. "Don't go."

She handed everyone a paper plate. "Have some food."

While Polly's friends were eating jelly and ice cream, Yuck came running in. "We're still hungry. Can we have some more food?" he asked.

"No," Polly said. "Go away."

"You've had yours, Yuck," Mum said. "We don't want you being sick."

Yuck sneaked off and took a look in the kitchen.

On a huge plate on the table was the big chocolate birthday cake. And on its top the word POLLY was written in icing, with icing sugar sprinkled over it.

It looked very tasty.

"Wow!" the others said when he came back upstairs.

He placed the cake on his bedroom floor.

"Won't Polly mind?" Little Eric asked.

"We'll just have one slice each," Yuck said, "and then we'll put it back."

But the cake was REALLY tasty.

"Maybe one more slice won't hurt," Fartin Martin said, passing the cake round again.

They were onto their fourth slice each when Mum knocked on the door.

"Have you seen Polly's cake?" she called.

Everyone looked at the plate on Yuck's floor. There was nothing but crumbs left.

Yuck held the door closed. "It's not in here, Mum," he said.

"What are we going to do?" Tom Bum whispered.

"We're going to be in BIG TROUBLE," Little Eric said.

"Quick, help me," Yuck told them. He grabbed the bucket from Pass the Mud. "Fill it with anything you can find."

Yuck poured the maggots from the Disgusting Dip into the bottom of the bucket. Tom Bum squeezed in some toothpaste. Fartin Martin dripped in some slug slime.

Little Eric scraped up his sick from the floor.

Everyone stared.

"Are you sure?" Tom Bum asked.

SPLAT! In it went.

Yuck sloshed everything around, churning the mixture with his hand. "We need something chocolatey."

They threw in handfuls of mud.

Yuck took down the Bubblegum Burp Balloons and dropped them in. **BURP! BURP! BURP!** Fartin Martin pulled a spider's web from his pants and dropped that in. Tom Bum stirred the mixture with his scab on a stick. Little Eric added some toenail clippings then scraped the slime from his head.

"Cheesy slime," he said.

Then Yuck plopped in some ketchup and bogeys and a final scoop of mud. The mixture was a thick chocolate brown.

Yuck turned the bucket upside down onto the plate and patted the bottom.

He lifted the bucket off, and there it was… Polly's brand new birthday cake.

On the top of the cake he wrote POLLY in toothpaste.

Then he shook his head over it, sprinkling dandruff like icing sugar.

"Good enough to eat," Fartin Martin said.

"Wait. A birthday cake should have candles," Little Eric said.

Yuck took a pot from beside his bed.

It was marked YUCK'S EARWAX – DO NOT TOUCH.

He scooped a handful of wax from the pot. It was yellow with brown bits in it. He rolled the earwax into candles and put a piece of string in the top of each. Then he tiptoed downstairs to the kitchen, put the new cake in the fridge and ran back up to his room.

It was Dad who found it.

"It's in the fridge, dear!"

"Oh, how lovely," Mum said, "you've added some candles. Polly will be thrilled."

Polly smiled as Mum and Dad carried the cake into the living room.

Her friends gathered round in a circle…

"Happy Birthday to you! Happy Birthday to you! Happy Birthday dear Polly! Happy Birthday to you!"

The candles flickered and sputtered bright green flames.

Polly took a deep breath and...
"Make a wish, Polly!" Juicy Lucy said.
Polly closed her eyes, and blew.

"I wish everyone would stay," she said.

"You're not meant to say it out loud or it won't come true," Emily Brush told her.

Yuck, Little Eric, Tom Bum and Fartin Martin crept down to the living room door and watched as Mum cut everyone a big slice of cake.

"There's a piece for each of you," Polly said, handing the plates out.

Yuck giggled in the doorway.

"What are YOU doing here, Yuck?" Polly said to him. "You're not invited!"

"I just came to say Happy Birthday," Yuck told her.

"Well, you can't have any cake," Polly said. "It's ALL for us!"

Yuck smiled as a slice of cake wriggled on Polly's plate.

"Eat up, everyone," Polly said. "I made it myself."

Yuck watched as one by one each of Polly's friends took a bite.

Their noses curled upwards.

Cake slithered through their fingers. It crawled from their nostrils and wriggled down their chins.

Their cheeks filled as they retched.

Madison Snake was sick over the Twinkletrout.

The Twinkletrout was sick over Megan the Mouth.

Megan the Mouth was sick over Spoilt Jessica.

Spoilt Jessica was sick over Juicy Lucy.

Juicy Lucy was sick over Clip-Clop Chloe.

Clip-Clop Chloe was sick over Emily Brush.

Emily Brush was sick over Madison Snake.

Polly was sitting in the middle.

"How does it taste?" Yuck asked her.

BLURGH!

Polly was sick over her presents.

"Did you eat too much, Polly?" Yuck asked.

But Polly didn't reply. Cake was crawling all over her face.

"That's gross," Yuck said. "What a GROSS PARTY!"

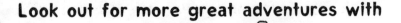